Andrea Salzman and Lacy Salzman

HOMESCHOOL PJ TiME

A Bedtime STEM Book

Illustrated by Amber West

COLBY
BOOKS™

This book is for my girl Lacy, who knew instinctively what was missing from each page. You are the reason it got done, Popsicle. —A.S.

For all the young, aspiring artists who passionately pursue their dreams. —A.W.

Text by Andrea Salzman and Lacy Salzman.
Illustrations by Amber West.

Paperback ISBN: 979-8-9858285-0-4
Hardcover ISBN: 979-8-9858285-1-1

Library of Congress Control Number: 2022918564

This is a work of fiction. Names, characters, places, and incidents either are the product of the author's imagination or are used fictitiously. Any resemblance to actual persons, living or dead, events, or locales is entirely coincidental.

Designed and typeset by Ryan Webb.
First edition 2022.

COLBY BOOKS™

Colby Books.
1143 Oak Ridge Turnpike #226, Oak Ridge, TN 37830 USA
www.colbybooks.com | www.homeschoolpjs.com | www.bedtimestem.com

Publisher's Cataloging-in-Publication data

Names: Salzman, Andrea, author. | Salzman, Lacy, author. | West, Amber, illustrator.
Title: Homeschool PJ time : a bedtime STEM book / by Andrea Salzman and Lacy Salzman; illustrated by Amber West.
Series: BEST Children's Book Series for Bedtime
Description: Oak Ridge, TN: Colby Books, 2022. | Summary: Nina Batina, homeschooler-at-large, loves doing school outside, learning kinetically. She plays junior scientist with friends, experimenting with Newton's Laws, art, chemistry. Includes bedtime STEM planner.
Identifiers: LCCN: 2022918564 | ISBN: 979-8-9858285-1-1 (hardcover) | 979-8-9858285-0-4 (paperback)
Subjects: LCSH Home schooling--Juvenile fiction. | Family life--Juvenile fiction. | Experiential learning--Juvenile fiction. | Science--Juvenile fiction. | Mathematics--Juvenile fiction. | Technology--Juvenile fiction. | Art--Juvenile fiction. | BISAC JUVENILE FICTION / School & Education | JUVENILE FICTION / Science & Nature / General | JUVENILE FICTION / Family / General
Classification: LCC PZ7.1.S2548 Ho 2022 | DDC [E]--dc23

First puddle jumping, skipping rocks –
It's Newton's law with dirty socks!

When boots crash down and mud **ERUPTs.**
The splatter gets a big thumbs-up.

The little brother
(aka Wild)

Secret File #C2W6

The sun goes down,
the dusk sublime . . .

It's Homeschool PJ
FIREFLY Time!

REACT TO ENVIRONMENTAL CHANGE
Want to hibernate like a firefly?
Time to burrow under the covers!

On **TUESDAY**,
Nina rolls from bed.

No bus today,
but **friends** instead.

Today she'll sketch,
compose, and play,

For Tuesdays are
her Meet-Up Day.

Her classmates map out Europe's shores.

A presentation she adores.

A Timeline Song
(sung way off-key),
then English, math,
astronomy.

All work is done,
the night sublime . . .

PHASES OF THE MOON
Can you whisper their names?
New, crescent, quarter, gibbous, full.

It's Homeschool PJ
MOON-WATCH
time!

Secret File #C2W11

On **WEDNESDAY**, Nina reads in bed.
No bus today, **THAT DOG** instead.

The world awaits, so much to see.
But what will her next lesson be?

The pool grows cold,
a fire sublime . . .

It's Homeschool PJ
MARSHMALLOW time.

HEAT FLOW
Rub your hands together. Does *Faster* equal *Warmer*?

Secret File #C2W23

On **THURSDAY**, Nina sings in bed.
No bus today, **THE ARTS** instead.

The words and music fill her mind.
They let her leave her world behind.

Her eyes are closed,
her mind alive.
She's humming
Ludwig's Number 5.

Now painting Monet
'neath the sky . . .
The greens so green,
they make her cry.

Secret File #C2W16 + 20

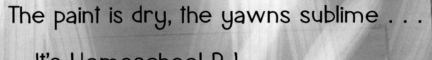

The paint is dry, the yawns sublime . . .

It's Homeschool PJ
TOOTHPASTE Time.

Secret File #C2W22

 WAYS LIGHT IS OBSERVED
Turn off the lights & shine a flashlight beam.
Can you make the light bounce?

On **FRIDAY**, Nina springs from bed.
No bus today, a **TRIP** instead.
Pack up a bag; pick up a friend.
The car-school options never end.

Potential rising to the top,

Awaiting a kinetic drop.

FORMS OF ENERGY

It's time to store some potential energy.
Close your eyes. Tomorrow is a BIG day.

The Scrambler
→

On **WEEKENDS,** Nina camps in bed.
No school today, a **FORT** instead.

Her brother
(Wild) plays
at her side,

While kittens (small)
seek ways to hide.

On **SATURDAY**, there's Momma talks,
A horseback ride, some Daddy walks.

Then all dressed up for **SUNDAY** praise—
two rest-filled, love-filled, simple days.

The week has passed, this life sublime . . .
It's Homeschool PJ
REPEAT Time.
REPEAT
REPEAT
REPEAT

**SCIENCE
TECHNOLOGY
ENGINEERING
MATHEMATICS**

Newton's 3rd Law Experiment

One idea: Put on your own boots. Step in a puddle gently. Was the **REACTION** small? Now stomp down and see if you get a bigger splash (maybe on brother).

Animal Reaction Experiment

One idea: Go on a bug hunt. Use a book or an "Insect ID" app to name your insects. Ask: How did this bug **react** differently to being caught than this other bug?

Heat Flow Experiment

One idea: Experiment with a sheet of aluminum foil, a white T-shirt, and a black T-shirt. Put all three in direct sunlight **(radiation)**. After fifteen minutes, which one is the hottest? What could make one hotter?

Light Observation Experiment

One idea: Get one flashlight, two small mirrors, and a friend. Turn off the lights and see if you can get the flashlight beam to **REFLECT** off both mirrors. Can you make the light bounce to every wall?

Forms of Energy Experiment

One idea: You don't need a giant roller coaster to play with **energy**. Climb the "littlest" slide at the playground and see how fast you slide down. Now try a bigger slide. Ask: Why is this slide more fun than that slide?

Weekly STEM Plan

On Monday, ...jumps from bed.

Write your name here

On Monday, Nina learned that "for every action, there will be an equal and opposite reaction". But she didn't truly understand **Newton's 3rd Law of Motion** until she found some puddles and started splashing. Nina learned best with her muck boots on!

MY MONDAY PLAN

Put your plan for Monday on a sticky note RIGHT HERE.

MY TUESDAY PLAN

Put your plan for Tuesday on a sticky note RIGHT HERE.

On Tuesday, ... rolls from bed.

Write your name here

On Tuesday, Nina began chasing fireflies, but she couldn't understand why so many lights were flashing in the dirt instead of the sky. So, she asked if fireflies **hibernate**. She found out that fireflies are beetles, not flies, and that females often have NO WINGS.

On Wednesday, ... reads in bed.

Write your name here

On Wednesday, Nina experimented with **heat transfer** to roast twelve marshmallows. Turns out, direct contact with flames **(conduction)** leads to lots of burned marshmallows! She discovered that marshmallows roast best in the heated air rising above the fire **(convection)**.

MY WEDNESDAY PLAN

Put your plan for Wednesday on a sticky note RIGHT HERE.

On Thursday, ... sings in bed.

Write your name here

On Thursday, Nina practiced making light bounce and bend by playing with a flashlight in the dark. She found that shining the beam onto the mirror makes light bounce **(reflection)** while shining the beam through a water glass makes it bend **(refraction)**. Naturally, her brother had an experiment of his own to perform.

MY THURSDAY PLAN

Put your plan for Thursday on a sticky note RIGHT HERE.

MY FRIDAY PLAN

Put your plan for Friday on a sticky note RIGHT HERE.

On Friday, ... springs from bed.

Write your name here

On Friday, Nina took her experiments to an amazing amusement park. She found out that roller coaster cars gain potential energy by climbing a massive hill. Once at the top, that **potential** is converted to **kinetic energy** . . . and the screaming can begin!

Predict the moon!
Ask how to track the phase of the moon when you go to bed tonight.

Do experiments with water!
Find out if water evaporates or freezes at different speeds when you add salt, sugar, or flour to it.

Paint a crazy idea!
Paint to Beethoven's 5th symphony and see what crazy artwork comes to life!

NOTE TO READERS

Bedtime STEM books are meant to be read twice, in quick succession. The first time through, let the rhyme and meter sweep you along. The second time around is perfect for interacting with the STEM boxes, while encouraging sleep behaviors. Once a week, it's time to plan! Get out the Sticky Notes and dream up your week, just like Nina!

ANDREA AND LACY SALZMAN live in a yellow house on a Zephyr Hill in East Tennessee. Andrea is motivated by children who need food and by coffee that needs creamer. Lacy, nearly nine, believes reading books out loud all day is normal behavior. She has never met an animal that did not deserve to live under her bed. Colby, age fourteen, loves baseball most of all. Andrea thanks the Good Lord and her husband Lee for the freedom to classically educate their children.

Homeschool PJ Time (www.homeschoolpjs.com) is the first in a series of Bedtime STEM books (www.bedtimeSTEM.com) designed to reinforce science concepts through bedtime stories about children who homeschool. Andrea can be reached at info@colbybooks.com.

AMBER WEST is a passionate, 15-year old artist who enjoys drawing, creative writing, and spending time with her horse. Her homeschool lifestyle has allowed her to develop a gift that has been evident to her family and close friends from a very young age. While she has done commission work for clients in traditional mediums before, this book was her first opportunity to produce artwork entirely from a digital platform. She enjoyed this new challenge and hopes that you also enjoy the art in Homeschool PJ Time. Amber may be reached at animalartbyamber@gmail.com.

Made in the USA
Coppell, TX
07 May 2024